The Art of Flying is Self-Inspiring!

Fly Like
Icarus!

Spontendor's Second Adventure

Yolanta Lensky

Print information available on the last page

Rev. date: 09/22/2015

To order additional copies of this book, contact:
Xlibris
1-888-795-4274
www.Xlibris.com
Orders@Xlibris.com

TABLE OF CONTENTS

Introduction..2

Part One

Asking Questions Is Fun! 5

Chapter 1

The Monument 7

Chapter 2

The Puzzle 9

Chapter 3

The Vision 11

Chapter 4

Toileting...13

Chapter 5

It is Fun to fly over the Sun! 15

Chapter 6

The Wizard's Plea to the Sun! 16

Chapter 7

The Heart Beat 18

Chapter 8

I Want to Conquer You, the Sun! 19

Chapter 9

"Beauty Adds Wings to Us!" 21

Part Two

Knowledge Put to Action Is Double Power! 24

Chapter 10

The Law of the Cause and Effect 25

Chapter 11

Wisdom is Power!..26

Chapter 12

Intuition is Our Ammunition! 28

Chapter 13

Apology is accepted!...29

Chapter 14

Flying on the Rainbow! 30

Conclusion

Nothing Is Impossible! 32

INTRODUCTION

1. The Overview of Book One

Hi, my dear friend! I hope you remember our first meeting in the book '**Spontendor, the Flying Baby-Horse"**. Do you remember your new friends: **Spontendor,** a flying baby-horse, a **Pegasus,** and his curly friend, **Princess Antoinette,** who was full of admiration for life and the beauty around her? Do you remember how in her **inspiration,** she kept saying **"Wow!"** all the time when she saw a beautiful flower or a colorful bird? This is how she expressed her **amazement** with the beauty of the Mother Nature! You admire it, too, right?

One day, Antoinette incidentally walked out of the gates of the ancient city on **Olympus** where she lived, and, of course, she got lost. Her father, **God Zeus,** was very upset and worried about her. He asked his little friend Spontendor to fly around the city, find his **curious** little daughter and bring her back home. Spontendor managed to find Antoinette by her Wows, and it was quite an adventure! Spontendor became a **Super-hero** for all the people on the Olimpus for his first **noble** deed.

In this book," **Spontendor's Second Adventure,"** you will get to know about another, quite an **amazing** and very knowledgeable **endeavor of** Spontendor's. He grew now into a 13-year-old Pegasus who could fly much higher, much **further,** and much faster than before. Spontendor's best friend, another amazing **mythological** character, Icarus, was inspired with the adventure of flying over the Sun. Wow! Picture that! That's really something very **daring**! Do you think it's possible to do it? **The myth** tells us that Icarus had an **ambition** to fly over the Sun **to empower** himself and the Sun! **Unfortunately**, he was burnt by the Sun that wouldn't let him do it. So, he fell down to the Earth and was turned into the monument. That is certainly very sad, but the story of Icarus is very **memorable** for people all over the world because it teaches us to fly in our minds and **to explore the unknown**. The questions why Icarus perished on that journey and what we can learn from his lesson are the ones that Spontendor wants to find an answer to in this book. Let's go on this adventure together with him!

NOTHING IS IMPOSSIBLE!

2. Massage Your Mind with New Words!

My dear little friend, reading is **also massaging your mind with new ideas and new words**. It is the best way to get to know some interesting things and learn new words that make you very smart! You definitely have paid attention to some words that are highlighted in the Introduction above. I have done it on purpose. I want you to learn all the **highlighted words** and use them when you are telling the story to your mom, sister, brother, your granny, grandpa, or your friends that do not have the book yet. Mind you, the language that this book is written in is the most used language in the world! *It is* *called the English language*. Be very proud of speaking in it! It is real fun to tell this story to someone using the words of the story that we have highlighted for you.

The best way to learn them is to take *a pack of index cards* and write each word on the back of a card. Use the face of a card *to draw the picture of a word*. *It's very* important *to indicate the part of speech* a word belongs to *(a noun, an adjective, an adverb, or a verb)* on each card. Ask your mom to help you discriminate the words for their function in speech. This knowledge will help you build up your *Language Skills* that will help you think in a very special way. *S*oon, you will have a whole pack of new words in your hands. It is your personal *Vocabulary!* *By the way, y*ou may play different *Language Games* with these cards:

a) *You may guess the word by **the capital letter** on the face of the card.*

a) *You may compete with a friend by the **number of the new words you learn.***

a) *You may **play in the parts of speech.** For instance, each of you comes up with a new **noun.** If you say a word that or **not a noun,** you failed. You can also play with the adjectives, or verbs. It's real fun!*

a) *Ask your mom to give you any of the words (let's call them **the key words**), and try to **make up any sentence** with them. If you read the book several times, you will for sure be able **to memorize the words** and remember the situations in which they were used better.*

THE MORE WORDS YOU KNOW, THE SMARTER YOU WILL BECOME!

3. You are Unique in Every Stance!

Are you intrigued? Do you feel like reading this book? Good, very good! Remember, my dear friend, all **unbelievable** things are done by brave, smart kids that keep asking the **Why questions** and get amazed at the **wonders** of the world. They are just like you!. You like to ask the Why questions, right? All **curious** and **inquisitive** kids do. The **myth** about Icarus keeps us asking the why questions and marveling at his courage still now. It makes us believe in the impossible!

IMAGINE, ICARUS CHARGED THE SUN! WOW!

His deed was so unique, so **incredible!** You are most unique, too, and you will also do something **outstanding** one day! I believe in you, my friend, and, therefore, I want you to say the magic words below out loud and learn them by heart. They will help you accomplish many wonderful things in life, in the same way as they helped Spontendor. They are called the **magic mind-sets!**

TO BE NEVER UPSET, CHANGE YOUR MIND-SET!

These magic mind-sets are about you, too, because **you are unique!** You are also one of a kind, like Spontendor, the Pegasus that you have come to befriend in my first book. Here are these magic words for you to prove that. Please learn them by heart and let them help you do something very special in life, too!

I am unique in every stance!

I was born, but only once!!

There isn't, there wasn't, there won't ever be

Anyone like me!!!

There is one more magic **mind-set** that Spontendor likes repeating to himself. He loves flying! So, he keeps boosting up his spirit with these words:

I defy the gravity of a common sense thought

And fly to the stars, no matter what!

Learn to Fly in your Mind!

You are one of a kind!

IN MY MIND, I AM ONE OF A KIND!
THERE WASN'T. THERE ISN'T,
THERE WON'T EVER BE
ANY ONE LIKE ME!

PART ONE

ASKING QUESTIONS IS FUN!

Ask and You will Be Answered!

CHAPTER 1

THE MONUMENT

It was a mystery date for Spontendor. On that day a year ago, Spontendor saw the body of Icarus, his best friend, flying straight to the Sun, as high as the eye could see. Unfortunately, in some time, the body of Icarus got burnt in the ruthless rays of the Sun, and it fell down to the earth. Then, constricted by effort, Icarus's body was turned into a monument.

Now, Spontendor was standing in front of that monument, lost in thoughts. It was so sad that Icarus didn't make the flight over the Sun! It was said he had tried too much. But Spontendor knew better. He knew that it was the qualities of real passion to conquer the unknown that cut his friend's life short. He was so brave, so special, so unbelievable!

Icarus had always been very curious about the Sun! He had a dream to fly over the Sun to see what there was behind it. He wanted to empower the Sun's unbeatable rays! Icarus stood up to the Nature's powers! He did not pursue the security of the qualities that simple pagan horses had to maintain. He was not a Pegasus; he was a human being! He was also different; he was unique! Icarus was able to do anything he wanted! That is why his favorite words were

I can ! I want to..., and I will!

Icarus could fly in the sky as high as possible, and he had no equal to him in flying! He had no one to compare with him, either, and that is why the Sun judged to take him.

Do some reasoning:

1. *What are your best qualities? What do you like about youself?*
2. *What can you do better than anyone? . Do you have any dreams?*
3. *What were Icarus's favorite words?*

Mind you!

Dreams create you and the world around you, too!

CHAPTER 2

THE PUZZLE

The season was autumn. However, the temperatures were high, and kids refused to prepare the crops for the winter. The elders said that the Sun was mounting. Last year, in October, the nose of Icarus was buried as the only remains of his that the Sun hadn't turned into ashes.

Suddenly, Spontendor felt disturbed. He sat down and stood up, sat down and stood up again. He walked and pondered, walked and pondered over the reasons of Icarus's failure. Icarus was a little older than Spontendor. He was more mature. He should have known better!

Why? Why? Why did the Sun turn him to ashes? Where did he go wrong on his flight? Why was the Sun so merciless to him? Spontendor missed Icarus so much that he frowned at the Sun each time he stepped into it in the morning. He blamed the Sun for his friend's death. But he was determined now more than ever to find out the truth. So, he kept repeating to himself:

I can find out the truth!

I want to find out the truth, and

I will find out the truth!

Mind you!

You can do whatever you want to if you do it with passion!

CHAPTER 3

THE VISION

Last July was the month of the **spectacular** flight that Icarus had undertaken. It was always in July that Icarus and Spontendor were training to overcome the fear of flying higher, higher, and higher, closer, closer, and closer to the Sun.

"Oh, God!" Spontendor sighed. "**How** great those days were! He will never, ever forget their **fantastic** flights over the tallest trees, hills, mountains, **cliffs,** clouds, and stars! Wow! They had flown everywhere, and it was real fun! But, one day, Icarus made the fight without Spontendor, and he never came back. Nothing had ever happened to him when they were together. Why wouldn't Icarus have taken me with him?" Spontendor wondered again and again. Every time that Spontendor thought about Icarus, his heart started racing in the fashion that it did when they used to fly together through the clouds in the sky, pretending to conquer the space and time. It was so **awesome!**

-"Pretense", experience", Spontendor muttered to himself. Those were the words that Icarus liked to say when he was talking to himself, planning his exciting journey." *I can, I want to, and I will*!" Spontendor repeated the favorite words of Icarus to himself again and again.

- That's right, said a voice behind him. "Pretense, experience. *I can, I want to, and I will!*"

Spontendor startled. He looked around. There was no one. He drank some water from his bowl and splashed some of it on his nose. **Wow! It's intriguing now!**

-"Pretense, experience", he heard again. Suddenly the shadow of Icarus covered his **entire** body. Spontendor jumped up, his heart ready **to burst out**. He recognized the voice of his friend. He **galloped** around the place, but there was no one.

Do some reasoning:
1. *Who do you think that was?*
2. *What words did Spontendor hear? Why them?*

Mind you!

Put the Letter "T" before the Letter "A"
Think before Acting!

CHAPTER 4

TOILETING

That night Spontendor was doing his regular toileting before going to bed. As soon as he was getting ready to brush his main, a prudish shape of Icarus surfaced again over him and said, "You don't lunge right." "Excuse me, who is here? Spontendor felt his navy colored brush get stuck in his main that fell untangled by the shadow's presence.

- "Pretense, experience' the shadow said and disappeared in the dark. Then he heard the words at a distance: *I can..., I want to..., and I will...!* What did the shadow want to tell Spontendor? Why was it there? Does Icarus want him to do something?

Do some reasoning:

1. *Do you know whose shadow it was? What's your guess?*
2. *Why did Spontendor hear the words "I can...; I want to..., and I will...!"*

Mind you!

Do everything with precision!

CHAPTER 5

IT IS FUN TO FLY OVER THE SUN!

The next morning, Spontendor went to speak to the Tacoma tree wizard who knew everything. The wizard had helped him on his first adventure. The wizard always sat under the tree, the vines of which ran up as high as 500 light years. The Tacoma tree was the main attraction of all their flights. Any point in the sky that they had ever flown to together with Icarus was reflected in its leaves that mainly fed only cows. They could dream endlessly in the shadow of that magic tree. The rays of the Sun, peeping through its leaves, had enticed Icarus to fly over the Sun and conquer it. What fun it was to look up through the leaves at the sky and imagine flying between them on the beams of the sun rays! They often lay under the tree in the shade and fantasized about their flights.

Suddenly, Spontendor heard the voice that echoed, "It is fun to fly over the Sun!" Icarus used to sing these words on and on," Spontendor recalled. "Wait a second, what does Icarus's voice want to tell me? **Why did he appear again?** Spontendor wondered "There must be some sacred meaning in that, "he mused.

Do some reasoning:

1. *Why did Icarus rhyme the word "fun" with the word "the Sun"?*
2. *2. Great! You got it! You are really expanding your thinking!*

Mind you!

Asking questions is fun, right?

CHAPTER 6

THE WIZARD'S PLEA TO THE SUN!

When the Sun came into the zenith, the wizard addressed the Sun in a very respectful fashion. "God Sun, Ra, "he began. This is how everyone addressed the Sun in those days.

- "Your sharpness has dried our tears for Icarus that you had turned into ashes. What had he done to outrage you so? He was the bravest of the brave among us! Please, Honorable, God Ra, do not disturb Icarus's monument with your heat now. His noble deed is in our hearts. Please, go back on your route. We shall need your bright light no longer today. "But if I lessen my shine, the kids will play less in my absence," the Sun replied in a very tired voice..

Spontendor was perplexed with the Sun's response. His head was in a swirl from the pounding question which the wizard did not even ask the Sun. Why had God Ra destroyed his friend? Why had God Ra left the question unanswered? Even the wizard couldn't make the Sun grant them an answer.

- "True, Spontendor reasoned further." The Sun is right that kids always get out of control when it is not shining. They get bored and cranky. But then again, what does this fact have to do with Icarus? He is never coming back... Should he leave probably the Sun alone, and let it shine on, as it had done for millennia?"

Do some reasoning:

1. *Is the Sun to blame for having burnt Icarus? What do you think?*
2. *Do you also feel bored without the Sun shining in the sky?*
3. *Why did the wizard call Icarus's flight noble?*
4. *Why didn't the Sun want Icarus to fly over it? Any ideas?*

Mind you!

Any noble deed is great, indeed!

CHAPTER 7

THE HEART BEAT

However, Spontendor could not stop thinking about Icarus. He had to know why his friend couldn't have realized his dream. He even started hating the Sun and avoiding its luminous rays that he and Icarus had admired so much before. Not that he didn't love being in the Sun altogether. Not at all! He admitted inwardly that everything looked so colorless and dull without it. However, he did not feel the joy of being in the sun any more.

- I miss, you, Icarus, I miss you", Spontendor muttered out loud, his heart pounding in unison, faster and faster.

:-"Fun in the Sun; fun in the Sun; fun in the Sun"... He heard the voice of Icarus over his head.

-I miss you, I miss you! I miss you" Spontendor repeated in response. No one answered this time. His heart kept racing: 21, 21,21.../ 21, 21, 21.../ 21,21,21...

That's the beat of your heart, too, my friend It is beating fast, but very rhythmically. Just put your right hand on your chest on the left side and listen to its beat: 21, 21, 21... Do your hear it? Isn't it amazing?! It's like the beat of the words:" *Fun in the Sun; fun in the Sun; fun in the Sun!*" Check out these words, too. Isn't this rhythm amazing? No doubt Icarus loved it! Then he heard,

I can..., I want to..., and I will...!

Spontendor started flying high up in the air, singing these words because they connected him to Icarus in his heart. The sadness that filled his heart was finally blown away by the loving beat of his heart. It united him with Icarus in it.

Do some reasoning:
1. *Why did Spontendor avoid being in the Sun??*
2. *What is the loving beat of your heart?*

Mind you!

Listen to your heart; it talks to you!
If something ever goes wrong, be calm, determined, and very strong!

CHAPTER 8

I WANT TO CONQUER YOU, THE SUN!

The next morning, the Sun was very bright again, and the kids were joyfully playing in it. Spontedor stepped out into the blazing Sun, his upper feet high up in the air. He looked tall and confident like that. Then he looked up, straight into the Sun's eyes and said challengingly,

- God Sun , Ra! My mind desires to conquer you!" I will fly over you, like Icarus wanted to do! I will!

-"Don't you have your fear bent up after the way Icarus failed."

– "No, I don't "I keep repeating his motto, and it helps me overcome my fear!

- " I am applauding to your enthusiasm. Good luck with your inspiration," said the Sun and doubled its glee. Spontendor's eye beams stopped to sparkle. He put his front feet down, one after the other in dismay.

 "Oh, I know what I have to do." Spontendor reasoned out," I need to protect myself." He went straight to the place where they rang a special Pegasus bell. It was ebonized. Ebonizing was the ultimate protection used on the bells." Icarus had ebonized his wings before his flight. "I'll get my wings ebonized, too; that's for sure", Spontendor professed. He felt again determined and strong.

I can! I want to...! And I will!

"Why on earth", he thought, "should he be scared? He suddenly felt the stratospheric happiness at the thought of his flight to the Sun. Just that thought had made Icarus hilariously happy, too. Spontendor felt deep down that happiness that had inspired Icarus was filling him up, and it was such a magnificent feeling!

Do some reasoning:

1. *Why did Spontendor feel suddenly hilariously happy?*

Mind you!

Be inspired with your dreams! Never give up on them!

CHAPTER 9

"BEAUTY ADDS WINGS TO US!"

That day Spontendor went to see his main advisor - Princess Antoinette, his second best friend, who had never said "Wow!" without the sun shining through her beautiful curls, like through the leaves on the Trachoma tree. Antoinette was the girl who had the sun in her heart and its beauty in her vision. She was always hilariously happy! Her endless wows expressed her admiration for the beauty of the Mother Nature that she saw everywhere. Antoinette always said,"

"Beauty adds wings to me! I want to fly to see it from above!

How well Spontendor understood Antoinette now! "She, for sure, will be the one to share his feelings with," he thought. "She would know how to conquer the Sun! She has enthusiasm, happiness, and beauty. And then, of course, she loves to fly". Spontendor flew up into the air and started circling around the Olympus, listening carefully where the happy wows could be were coming from. Antoinette must be somewhere around. Oh! There she is, among those roses that are growing in the royal garden. Antoinette admired their colors and the scent, repeating, "Wow! Wow! Wow! You are so incredibly beautiful!"

- "Hi, Princess Antoinette, I have come to propose that we complete for the human ability to fly over the Sun!" Spontendor declared with pride. Then he added,

"I can do it! I want to do it! And I will do it!"

Antoinette wiped her beautiful eyes from the morning glory dew that fell from the royal flowers, growing everywhere, even next to her bed, and then said,

- "That's a very honorable desire", but do you know how to be present in every moment and how to treasure every minute?

- "No, I don't think so," said Spontendor. "But I count every flap of my wings, and I enjoy every click of my horseshoes. Does that count?

- Do you know how to be happy around the Sun and see its blazing beauty in every flower?

- Not yet, confessed Spontendor, but I can learn that ,too!

- Do you know how **to salute** to knowledge and grasp every **speck** and **whack of reality** to learn more about it**?**

- "No, I don't think so...., but I can learn that, too!

- "O. K. I'll help you. But, let's do some learning first. I need to see **Goddess Andromeda** and ask her about the secrets of the Sun and its unique qualities first. She knows everything about the stars and **the cosmic laws.** Her **wisdom** is endless. I'll talk to her and get some wisdom for both of us. She is very **wise.** Come to see me tomorrow. We'll make up a plan together".

Do some reasoning:

1. *Why did Princess Antoinette ask Spontendor those questions?*
2. *What did she want him to learn and why?*
3. *Was Spontendor ready to learn the new things?*
4. *What is the last new thing that you have learnt?*

Mind you!

Never stop learning!

A great man whose name is **Albert Einstein** *had an amazing imagination, and we have many wonderful things thanks to him, your smart phone, for example. He always said to the kids that lived nearby,*

"Fertilize your Mind with Thinking!"

END OF PART ONE

PART TWO

KNOWLEDGE PUT TO ACTION IS DOUBLE POWER!

What you can do and want to do,
You, certainly, Will do!

CHAPTER 10

THE LAW OF THE CAUSE AND EFFECT

Spontendor went back home hoping that Antoinette will figure out what to do after her talk with Goddess Andromeda. He had a huge respect for the wisdom of Goddess Andromeda who had been supervising Antoinette since birth and who had taught her many wonderful things. In the morning, he went to the dreadful spot where Icarus fell down, the place that had his monument now.

"I know why you wanted to fly over the Sun, but I don't know why the Sun wouldn't let you do that! " Spontendor said, talking to the monument. "I want to repeat your flight and find out the cause of your failure. Tell me what it was? "

-"The cause, cause, cause", echoed the voice in the distance. *The body in motion stays in motion.* " Spontendor turned around, but he heard nothing. There was chilling silence around. ." So, the cause has something to do with Icarus's motion", he concluded. "Something must have been wrong with it. But what was wrong?" Spontendor flew to see Antoinette as swiftly as he could. Maybe she had the answer.

Do some Reasoning:

1. *What did Icarus want to tell Spontendor?*
2. *Why did he mention the word "motion"?*

Mind you!

Always go to the cause of your actions to make no mistakes in them!

CHAPTER 11

WISDOM IS POWER!

Antoinette was sitting in her royal garden alone, waiting for Spontendor. "Darling Lady," Spontendor began talking to her.. "The spirit of Icarus that is wondering now in the plains up there somewhere came to see me again, and it told me that his unfortunate flight had something to do with motion."

"Yes, I know", Antoinette retorted. "Goddess Andromeda explained everything to me. She says that the Sun is the center of our solar system in the Milky Way galaxy, and it is millions of light years away from us and from the other stars. "The Sun is a Star itself," she continued, "and it is very, very powerful! It can burn anything that gets close to it. That's why we cannot stay in the Sun for too long.

–"It is very, very, very hot!", Antoinette continued, "and its energy consumes anything and anyone that gets near its hemisphere. No one can fly over the Sun! That's why Icarus got burnt. Goddess Andromeda thinks that the Sun liked Icarus's ambition to fly over it, but it knew all along that he would be punished for his ignorant desire to conquer the unconquerable.

"Wow! That's amazing! "Spontendor said in admiration. " I know now that it is impossible to be done, and it feels so good to understand why. We really owe this knowledge to Icarus! If it were not for him, we would never get to know that The Sun is the star".

-" But, wait", Antoinette continued. "It's not all. Goddess Andromeda says that the body of Icarus had got burnt, but its energy is still in motion. That is why his spirit, which is just the energy of his body, comes down teaching us something."

– "Wow! That explains it," said Spontendor. "You have solved the puzzle for me why Icarus had fallen down. Thank you so much for your help! I like knowledge, and I know now why we need it. I want to fly to the sky as high as I can manage and apologize to God Ra for my ignorance, anger, and frustration.

-"That's exactly what Goddess Andromeda told me you should do." said Antoinette. "Why don't we do it together? I'd like to fly to the Sun and thank it for its beauty and the light that makes everything so wonderfully glamorous!

- "I love that idea!" said Spontendor, " But let's reason out every detail of our flight first. We cannot repeat the mistakes that Icarus had made. His daring flight has taught us a lot, and we should honor his courageous deed with wise actions."

Do some reasoning:

1. *Why couldn't Icarus reach the Sun? What is the Sun in our galaxy?*
2. *How long does it take to fly to the Sun?*

Mind you!

Always learn from your mistakes!

CHAPTER 12

INTUITION IS OUR AMMUNITION!

So, you see, my friend, all we have to do to realize our dreams is to learn more about the world around us and explore it with passion. There is also one more quality that you absolutely need to develop in order to do that. It is very precious, and it is called intuition. You have it deep in your heart. Everyone has it, but it needs to be heard and developed. Let's listen to what Antoinette has to tell Spontendor about it.

When Spontendor came to see Antoinette the next morning, he felt very inspired and confident that they would fly to the Sun in memory of his friend's incredible flight. He needed to apologize to the Sun for having blamed it unknowingly for Icarus's failure to conquer it. Antoinette was impatiently waiting for Spontendor. "Goddess Andromeda has told me", she started, "that we have to listen to what our intuition tells us first. She says that intuition is our inner voice that protects us from harm. It always directs us in the realization of our dreams. We just need to listen to it very carefully.

-"Oh, yes, I know what you mean! "Spontendor jumped into the air." I have it! I have this inner voice in me! It tells me that we need to plan our flight on the day of Icarus's birthday! Why don't we do it on that day? It will happen tomorrow. That's probably why the spirit of Icarus comes to visit me every day." -"Great intuition", exclaimed Antoinette. "And I have my revelation, too. Let's fly to the Sun on the Rainbow! Goddess Andromeda says that it comes out in the sky to connect the Earth and the Sun, like a bridge. We'll follow its route and enjoy the beauty of the rainbow that I love to draw so much!"

"Wow! I love your intuition! Let's figure out every detail of our flight in the time and space! It will be the best birthday gift for Icarus! That's a great idea!

Do some Reasoning:

1. *Do you like to draw rainbows, my friend? Why?*

Mind you!

Listen to your heart!
Make your Heart Smart
and the Mind Kind!

CHAPTER 13

APOLOGY IS ACCEPTED!

" I observed the rainbow so many times", Antoinette began her reasoning. "The Sun is most charming and welcoming after the rain, when one part of the sky is still in the clouds, but the other part opens up for the Sun to peep in through them. It's then that the rainbow miraculously colors the sky. We have to catch that moment. It doesn't last long!"

-"You are right! The mushrooms start growing like crazy after such rain. I love the smell of them in the air! Now I know why you asked me if I could live in the present moment and enjoy every second of it. Let's catch that moment!"

- "Right! That's what I meant. Now, let's watch the sky. It is sure going to rain after all that unbearable heat. The Sun must be exhausted to have been blazing for days on end."

- "I know what I have to do to lessen its anger. I will apologize to it right away!".

Spontendor immediately stood up onto his back legs, stretched the front ones forward and said out loud and very confidently and very respectfully,

- "God Sun Ra! Please, accept my apologies! I didn't know better when I accused you of Icarus's failure to conquer you. You are unconquerable! I know now that you are the center of our solar system Thank you for the light that you are shedding on us! Thank you for the beauty that you generate around us! We love you!" Suddenly, the Sun hid behind a big cloud and a nice warm rain began to fall down on the Earth. Spontendor kneeled down to let Antoinette climb up onto his back, his heart pounding again in unison with hers: 21.21.21.../ 21,21,21.../ 21, 21, 21!

Do some reasoning

1. *Is your heart pounding now? Why? When does it pound very, very fast?*
2. *Did the Sun forgive Spontendor? How come?*

Mind you!

Conquer the unconquerable!

CHAPTER 14

FLYING ON THE RAINBOW!

In a few moments, the Sun came out from behind the clouds, very warm and forgiving. Spontendor and Antoinette saw a magnificent rainbow crossing the sky with a fantastic array of colors! Spontendor launched into the air, and they flew up into the clouds, following the magic route of the rainbow in ecstasy.

"Thank you, thank you, and thank you!!!"

The voice came after them from afar. Icarus was hilariously happy with them! Antoinette and Spontendor had their amazing trip in time and space on the date of Icarus's birthday, and from that day on, they called that moment

"The Now moment, or the magic moment because every Now moment is magic!"

Wow! We are flying on the rainbow now!

CONCLUSION

NOTHING IS IMPOSSIBLE!

Thus, my darlings, this story ends, but its spirit will stay with us forever. It is teaching us to value what we have in the moment. The Now Moment tells us much about our planet Earth, and it reminds us to always trust our intuition.

Remember, every action has a reaction!

This rule teaches you to be responsible for your actions and to put your whims aside when it comes to what is in the light of the best qualities of life: *honesty and courage!* I am sure that one day you will embark on a fantastic voyage of a great scientific discovery yourself. It will bring you to the brink of knowing something that is now unknown. Icarus did not know the secret of the Sun, but his heroic deed was great, anyway. He posed the magic question.

Why? Only those that ask this question find the magic answers!

This question will take you on to the flights to other planets and galaxies, and you will owe that to Icarus, his wonderful dream, and his true friends that helped him realize his dream.

Good luck, my dear friend, on your future endeavors! I am sure they will be wonderful! Remember the magic mind-sets you've learnt in this book. Be incredible!

See you on the next adventure of Spontendo , your new Super-Hero!

Lovingly and with a great faith in you,

Yolanta Lensky

Fly in Your Mind!
You are One of a Kind!

Our mind's vital descriptions
Are like the prescriptions!
They keep us from dismay
Between "I Can!" and "I May!"

Printed in the United States
By Bookmasters